# THE WIND IN THE WILLOWS

## The River Bank

*Re-told by Anne McKie. Illustrated by Ken McKie.*

The Mole had been working very hard all the morning, spring-cleaning his little room. First with brooms, then with dusters; then on ladders and steps and chairs, with a brush and a bucket of whitewash. There were splashes of paint all over his black fur, his poor back ached and his arms were tired.

Spring was in the air! Mole could feel it, even in the dark depth of his little house underground.

Suddenly, he threw his brush down on the floor. "Bother!" he said. "Oh blow! Hang spring-cleaning!" and bolted out of his house without even waiting to put his coat on.

Once in the steep little tunnel outside his front door, he scrabbled and scratched and scraped, working busily with his little paws and muttering to himself, "Up we go! Up we go!" till at last, pop! his snout came out into the sunlight and he found himself rolling in the warm grass of a great meadow.

"This is fine!" he said to himself. "This is better than whitewashing!"

The warm spring sunshine and the soft breeze made the Mole jump for joy. With the sound of happy bird song in his ears, Mole went on his way across the meadow until he came to a gap in the hedge on the far side.

"Stop!" said an elderly rabbit at the gap. "Sixpence to use our private road!" But he was bowled over by Mole as he trotted by.

On and on through the meadows he wandered, along the hedgerows, across the copses until, suddenly, he stood by the edge of a river.

Never in his life had he seen a river before. It chuckled and gurgled, the water all glints and gleams and sparkles. Mole was bewitched.

He trotted along by the side of the river until he was quite tired out. Then he sat on the bank while the river clattered on.

As he sat on the grass and looked across the river, a dark hole in the bank opposite, just above the water's edge, caught his eye. "What a nice snug house that would make!" thought Mole dreamily.

As he gazed, something bright and small seemed to twinkle in the hole. Then, to his surprise, it winked, and Mole saw it was an eye. Gradually a small face appeared. A brown little face with whiskers, small neat ears and thick silky hair. It was the Water Rat!

Then the two animals stood and looked at each other.

"Hello, Mole!" said the Water Rat.

"Hello, Rat!" said the Mole.

"Would you like to come over?" asked the Rat.

"How can I do that?" said Mole rather crossly, for he knew nothing at all about riverside life and its ways.

The Rat said nothing, but stooped down and unfastened a rope and pulled on it; then stepped into a little blue and white boat - just the size for two animals.

Then the Rat rowed smartly across the river and tied up. He held out his paw as the Mole stepped gingerly down. "Lean on that!" he said. "Now then, step lively!" and the Mole, to his surprise, found himself actually sitting in a real boat.

"This has been a wonderful day!" said Mole, as the Rat rowed away. "Do you know, I've never been in a boat before in all my life!"

"What?" cried the Rat, open-mouthed. "Never been in a boat - what have you been doing then?"

"Is it so nice as all that?" asked the Mole, shyly. Then he leaned back in his seat and looked at the cushions and the oars, and lots of interesting things as the boat swayed gently under him.

The Water Rat leaned forward on his oar and said solemnly, "Believe me, my young friend, there is nothing - absolutely nothing - half so much worth doing as simply messing about in boats. Simply messing," he went on dreamily, "messing-about-in-boats."

"Look ahead, Rat!" cried Mole suddenly. It was too late. The boat struck the bank at full tilt, and the Rat lay at the bottom of the boat, with his heels in the air.

How the two friends laughed as the Rat picked himself up. "Look here!" said Rat to Mole. "If you've really nothing else to do this morning, why don't we row down the river together, and have a long day of it?"

The Mole waggled his toes from sheer happiness, sighed and leaned back into the soft cushions. "What a day I'm having!" he said. "Let's start at once!"

"Just a minute," said the Rat, as he tied up the boat to a ring on his landing-stage. Then he climbed up into his hole in the river bank. After a short while he came out carrying a very heavy wicker picnic-basket.

"Shove that under your feet," he said to the Mole as he passed it down into the boat.

"What's inside it?" asked the Mole, wriggling with curiosity.

"There's cold chicken inside it," replied the Rat: "Coldtonguecoldhamcoldbeefpickledgherkinssaladfrenchrollscress sandwichespottedmeatgingerbeerlemonadesodawater" -

"Oh stop, stop!" cried the excited Mole. "This is too much!"

"Do you really think so?" asked the Rat seriously. "It's only what I always take on these little river trips."

The Mole never heard a word he was saying, he was far too busy enjoying all the different scents and sounds of the river. As the Water Rat rowed quietly along, Mole dreamily trailed a paw in the water.

After a while, Rat began to tell Mole all about his life by the river. "It's my world, and I don't want any other!"

"But isn't it a bit dull at times?" asked Mole, timidly. "Just you and the river and no one else to talk to?"

"No one else!" the Rat laughed. "There are far too many people sometimes. Otters, kingfishers, dabchicks, moorhens, around and about all day long!"

"What lies over there?" asked Mole, waving his paw towards the dark woodland across the meadow.

"That's the Wild Wood," said Rat. "We don't go there very much, we river bankers."

"Aren't they - very nice people in there?" asked the Mole, nervously.

"Well," replied the Rat, "let me see. The squirrels are all right, but the rabbits are a mixed lot. And then there's Badger, who lives right in the heart of it. Dear old Badger! Nobody interferes with him. They'd better not!"

"Why, who should interfere with him?" asked Mole.

The Rat hesitated, then explained. "There are others. Weasels - and stoats - and foxes - and so on. They're alright in a way - but they break out sometimes, there's no denying it, and then you really can't trust them, and that's the fact."

"And beyond the Wild Wood again?" Mole asked, "where it's all blue and dim, and you can see what may be hills or the smoke of towns, or just clouds?"

"Beyond the Wild Wood comes the Wild World," said the Rat. "And that's something that doesn't matter to you or me. I've never been there and I'm never going, nor you, either, if you've got any sense at all! Now then! Here's our backwater at last, where we're going to have lunch!"

Leaving the main part of the river, they floated through to a little lake. Grassy green banks sloped down on either side. Brown snaky tree-roots gleamed below the surface of the quiet water. Ahead of them the water tumbled over a weir that drove a dripping mill wheel. It was so beautiful that Mole could only hold up both front paws and gasp, "Oh my! Oh my! Oh my!"

The Rat brought the boat alongside the bank, tied her up, helped Mole safely ashore, and lifted out the picnic-basket.

The Mole begged to be allowed to unpack it all by himself. Rat was pleased to let him while he stretched full length on the grass for a rest.

Very excited, Mole shook out the tablecloth and spread it, then he took out all the mysterious packets one by one and arranged their contents in order, still gasping, "Oh my! Oh my!"

When all was ready, the Rat said, "Now pitch in, old fellow!" which Mole gladly did, for he had started his spring-cleaning very early that morning, and it had been a very long time since breakfast.

"What are you looking at?" Rat asked the Mole, when they had had enough to eat, and Mole's eyes were able to wander off the tablecloth a little.

"I am looking," said the Mole, "at a streak of bubbles that I see travelling along the surface of the water. That strikes me as funny!"

"Bubbles? Oho!" said the Rat laughing.

A broad glistening nose showed itself above the edge of the bank, and the Otter hauled himself out and shook the water from his coat.

"Why didn't you invite me?" the Otter asked Rat, as he went towards the food. "All the world seems to be out on the river today!" the Otter went on. "I came up here to try and get a moment's peace, and then I stumble upon you fellows!"

There was a rustle behind them, coming from a thick leafy hedge - suddenly a stripy head appeared.

"Come on, old Badger!" shouted the Rat.

The Badger trotted forward a couple of steps, then grunted, "H'm! company," and turned his back and disappeared from view.

"That's just the sort of fellow he is!" said Rat quite disappointed. "Simply hates company. That's the last we'll see of him today. Well, tell us who's out on the river?" the Water Rat asked Otter.

"Mr. Toad's out," replied the Otter. "In his brand new racing boat; new clothes, new everything!"

The Water Rat smiled. "Once it was sailing, then it was punting, last year it was house-boating. It's always the same, whatever he does he soon gets tired of it, then starts on something fresh!"

From where they sat they could get a glimpse of the main stream of the river; just then a little racing boat flashed by with Mr. Toad rowing. He was short and stout, splashing badly and rolling all over the place. The Rat stood up and shouted to him, but Mr. Toad shook his head and sped on his way.

"He'll be out that boat in a minute if he rolls like that," said the Rat, sitting down.

"Of course he will," chuckled the Otter. "Did I ever tell you that story about Toad and the lock keeper?" Just then a Mayfly swooped low over the water...suddenly it had vanished - and so had the Otter. All that Mole could see of him was a streak of bubbles on the water.

"Well, well," said the Rat. "I suppose we ought to be moving. I wonder which of us had better pack the picnic-basket?"

"Oh, please let me," said the Mole. So, of course, Rat let him.

Packing the basket was not quite so pleasant work as unpacking it. It never is. But the Mole was quite determined to enjoy it. Just when he had got the basket packed and strapped up tightly, he saw a plate staring up at him from the grass. And when the job had been done again, the Rat pointed out a fork which one of them ought to have seen. Last of all, the mustard-pot, which Mole had been sitting on - and the job was finished!

The afternoon sun was setting low as Rat rowed gently homewards in a dreamy mood, murmuring poetry to himself, and not paying much attention to Mole.

By now the Mole was feeling quite at home in a boat (or so he thought) and was getting a bit restless. "Ratty! Please. I want to row now!"

The Rat shook his head with a smile. "Not yet, my young friend," he said. "Wait till you've had a few lessons. It's not as easy as it looks."

Mole was quiet for a minute or two. But he began to feel more and more jealous of Rat, rowing so strongly and so easily along. A small voice inside him began to whisper that he could do it just as well.

The Mole jumped up and seized the oars so suddenly that the Rat, who was gazing out over the water, was taken by surprise and fell backwards off his seat with his legs in the air. Swiftly, the Mole jumped in his place and grabbed the oars.

"Stop it, you silly fool!" cried the Rat, from the bottom of the boat. "You can't do it! You'll have us over!"

The Mole flung his oars back with a flourish, and made a great big dig at the water. He missed the surface altogether, his legs flew up above his head, and he found himself lying on the top of the poor Rat. Greatly alarmed, he made a grab at the side of the boat, and the next moment - Sploosh! over went the boat, and he found himself struggling in the river.

Oh my, how cold the water was, and oh, how very wet it felt. How it sang in his ears as he went down, down, down! How bright and welcome the sun looked as he rose to the surface coughing and spluttering! How afraid he was when he felt himself sinking again! Then a firm paw gripped him by the back of his neck. It was the Rat, and he was laughing. Mole could feel him laughing, right down his arm and through his paws and into his neck.

The Rat got hold of an oar and shoved it under the Mole's arm; then he did the same by the other side of him and, swimming behind, pushed the poor animal to shore, hauled him out, and set him down on the bank, a squashy, pulpy lump of misery.

When the Rat had rubbed him down a bit, and wrung some of the wet out of him, he said, "Now then, old fellow! Trot up and down on the bank as hard as you can, till you're warm and dry again, while I dive for the picnic-basket."

So the unhappy Mole, wet on the outside and ashamed on the inside, trotted about till he was fairly dry.

Meanwhile, the Rat dived into the water again, brought back the boat and tied her up. Then he dived for the picnic-basket and struggled to land with it.

When all was ready for a start once more, the Mole, sad and ashamed, took his seat in the stern of the boat. As they set off, he said in a trembling voice, "Ratty, my generous friend. I am very sorry indeed for my foolish and ungrateful behaviour. I almost lost that beautiful picnic-basket. I have been a complete fool, and I know it. Will you forgive me, and let things go on as before?"

"That's all right!" said Rat cheerily. "What's a little wet to a Water Rat? Look here, I think you'd better come and stop with me for a little while. I can make you comfortable - and I'll teach you to row, and to swim, and you'll soon be as handy in the water as any of us."

The Mole was so touched by Ratty's kind words that he could find no voice to answer him (and had to brush away a tear or two with the back of his paw).

But the Rat kindly looked away, and very soon the Mole felt happy again.

When they got home, the Rat made a bright fire in the parlour, and placed Mole in an armchair in front of it, having fetched down a dressing-gown and slippers for him.

Then the Rat told Mole river stories till supper time. Very thrilling stories they were too, to a Mole who had lived in a dark burrow all his life. Stories all about weirs and floods, leaping pike and herons. All about adventures down drains and night fishing with Otter.

Supper was a most cheerful
meal, but very shortly afterwards a
terribly sleepy Mole had to be taken
upstairs by the kind Water Rat.

Mole was given the best bedroom, where he soon laid his
head on his pillow quite happily knowing that his new found
friend, the River, was lapping the sill of his window.